Why Sun and Moon Live in the Sky

An African Legend

Why Sun and Moon Live in the Sky

An African Legend

AND OTHER FOLKTALES
Compiled by the Editors
of
Highlights for Children

CONTENTS

Why Sun and Moon Live in the Sky

An African Legend

Retold by Erika Mann

Once upon a time, long, long ago, Sun and Moon lived on earth. Sun was the husband, Moon was his wife, and all the Stars were their children. They had a beautiful house and many friends who often came to visit them. Their best friend, however, was Water, whom they visited quite often but who never visited them.

One day Moon said to her husband, "I cannot stand this any longer. What kind of friendship is this? Please, Sun, go and ask Water to come visit us."

Sun put on his best suit, went to the place where Water lived, and said, "My wife Moon asks you to come and visit us at our house. She is very grieved that you have not come."

"I would gladly come," said Water, "but you know our customs. If I bring my children and other relatives to your house, there will not be room enough for all of us. If you really want us to come, you will have to build another house, much, much bigger than the one you have now. It must be very big indeed."

Sun went home and told Moon, who was very glad to hear just why Water had not come to them before. So she and Sun and almost all the Stars (all that were big enough, anyway) got very busy and built the biggest house that had ever been seen. When it was ready—and it took quite a time to finish it—Sun again put on his best suit and went to Water to ask him to come.

Water listened and said, "All right. We shall come to your new house on Sunday at four o'clock and have tea with you."

Moon baked cakes and pies. Sun prepared sandwiches and biscuits. They swept the house, dusted it, and put fresh flowers everywhere. On Sunday all the Stars had their hair washed, their hands and faces scrubbed, and they even washed behind the ears. They put on their best clothes and waited impatiently for Water to come.

About three o'clock the light suddenly changed; there was a shine and a glimmer to it that had never been there before. Sun, Moon, and the Stars strained their eyes to see what was going on. Then they saw Water coming. He came with big waves and little waves, with shells and fish, crabs and turtles, starfish and jellyfish and seaweeds. He covered everything as he came nearer and nearer, until finally he reached the door of the beautiful house that Sun, Moon, and the Stars had built.

He greeted them and asked, "May we come in?"

"Certainly," replied Moon, "do come in."

So Water came in, and Sun, Moon, and the Stars found themselves wet to their ankles. Then Water said, "May some more of my family come in?"

Moon smiled as she said, "Of course, please tell them to come in."

So in came big waves and little waves, shells and fish, crabs and turtles, starfish and jellyfish and seaweeds. Sun, Moon, and the Stars were standing in company up to their waists. Sun and Moon picked up all their children and climbed up on chairs.

Then Water said, "Is there still room for some more of my family?"

9

Sun looked at Moon, and Moon looked at Sun, and then she said, "Yes, come in, make yourselves at home." But she did not smile any more.

Then, while more big waves and little waves, crabs and fish, shells and turtles, starfish and jellyfish and seaweeds came in, Sun made a hole in the roof and put all his children through it. Then Sun and Moon climbed out too and, holding each others' hands, they jumped again and again until they reached the sky.

When they looked down, their beautiful house had disappeared. There was only Water with big waves and little waves, shells and fish, crabs and turtles, starfish and jellyfish and seaweeds everywhere. So Sun built a new house in the sky, and that is where he and Moon and their children— the Stars—have lived ever since.

Oliver Tom and the Leprechaun

An Irish Folktale

Retold by Judy Cox

Oliver Tom Fitzpatrick was the oldest son of a farmer, and you'd not find a friendlier, more good-looking lad in the whole of county Kildare. Though if he were as clever as he was good-looking, I'd not be telling this story.

One bright morning when the bees were humming, Oliver Tom strolled down the lane on his way to market. He was taking his time, for no more effort would Oliver Tom put into a task than he knew he could get out again.

Away under the hedgerow he heard a noise: *Tick-tack, tick-tack.* Being country bred, he thought 'twas surprising to hear the birds singing so late in fall.

Tick-tack, tick-tack.

Quiet as an old yellow cat after a mouse, Oliver Tom edged through the bushes and peered into the green brambles. There he saw a wee, deeny, dawny bit of an old man, wearing a cocked hat and tapping his hammer against the sole of a tiny shoe for the mending of it.

Now Oliver Tom was not daft, and he knew he was watching a leprechaun. He scratched his chin and he scratched his head and he thought to him-self: *If I go quick to work, I'll be a rich man. For they do say if you catch a leprechaun, he must give you his pot of gold.*

"Top 'o the morning to you!" Oliver Tom says, coming closer to the little man. The little man put down his hammer and glared at Oliver Tom, all the while thinking how to make his escape.

"And the rest 'o the day to you," muttered the old man grudgingly.

"How goes the work?" Oliver Tom asked, moving closer.

"Might be fine, might be better," the leprechaun replied, giving Oliver Tom the eye. Suddenly, he looked over Oliver Tom's shoulder. "Saint's be!" he cried, "Aren't those cows wandering about in your father's ripe corn?"

Now Oliver Tom nearly forgot what he was about and turned to see, but then he remembered you mustn't take your eyes from a leprechaun for a minute. Quick as a wink, Oliver Tom leaped forward and caught the leprechaun up in his hand. "Now I've got you!" he cried.

"Put me down, you great ox!" the wee man yelled, struggling like a fish in Oliver Tom's hand. But Oliver Tom would not let him down.

"Show me to your pot of gold, for I know you've buried it nearby," Oliver Tom said.

After much pleading and fussing, the leprechaun agreed to lead Oliver Tom to his hoard of gold. Oliver Tom tied him up in his red handkerchief (to protect himself against biting) and set off as the leprechaun directed—up hills and down hills, over ditches and under hedges, across fields and streams, until at last they came to a great field of ragweed. There was row upon row of golden ragweed as far as the eye could see.

The wee little man pointed to a tall stalk of ragweed and said, "Dig under that stalk and you'll get a crock full of gold."

Oliver Tom untied the handkerchief and set the leprechaun down. He looked around the field, but nowhere, near or far, could he see something to dig with. "I must go back and get me shovel," he said. "But all the stalks look alike. How will I know where to dig when I get back?"

He scratched his chin and he scratched his head. Finally, he tied his red handkerchief around the ragweed stalk to mark the place to dig.

The leprechaun watched him. "Have you any more need of me, then?" the wee little man asked.

"No," said Oliver Tom. "You may go if you like. Godspeed to you, and may good luck attend you wherever you go."

"Well, good-bye to you, Oliver Tom," the leprechaun said. "And much good may it do you with what you find." With a wink and a bow the little man was gone.

Oliver Tom hurried home and got his shovel. Then he ran back—up hills and down hills, over ditches and under hedges, across fields and streams until at last he came to the same ragweed field. Tom stopped short and stared. His mouth popped open and his eyes grew wide with the seeing of it.

Stretching a good twenty Irish acres before him, Oliver Tom saw a field of waving red handkerchiefs, one on each yellow ragweed stalk. He struck his brow with his hand. "The leprechaun has played me false!" he cried. "I left me handkerchief to mark the spot where he told me to dig, and now every last stalk of ragweed is tied with a bit o' red!"

Well, Oliver Tom dug and he dug, under this bush and under that. And when the sun went down behind the hill, Oliver Tom was sitting in a field of holes. And no gold had he found, not so much as a pretty copper penny. And when at last he lay down his shovel and wiped his forehead with a red handkerchief, he had a great laugh and a little tear over the trick the leprechaun had played.

The Treasure of Our People

By David Lubar

Everyone had told her there was nothing to fear. In her heart, Tiana knew this was true. But her stomach didn't believe her heart. The unknown was scary. Many of her friends—all of her older friends—had already been through their First Passage. They wouldn't tell her anything about the experience. They would smile gently, but none would give her even the smallest clue.

Today, on the dawn following the first full moon after her birthday, was her turn. As Tiana thought these things, Wisemother Gayloris entered her hut.

"Greetings of the morning," the woman said.

"Greetings, Wisemother," Tiana replied.

Gayloris held out her hand and smiled. She was one of the seven who led the village, taught the people, and, when necessary, judged and punished. It was rarely necessary.

"Where are we going?" Tiana asked.

"To see the greatest treasure of our people."

Tiana felt her heart leap at these words. A treasure would not be frightening. It would be wonderful and beautiful. They walked, hand in hand, across a field to the edge of the woods.

"We go here," Gayloris said, pointing to a cave.

"There?" Tiana didn't like that idea.

"It is a short journey." The Wisemother took a torch that was leaning near the entrance of the cave and lit it with something in her hand. She walked into the mouth of the cave.

Tiana followed. In a few moments, she saw sunlight. Soon after, they came out on the side of a large hill. "Is the treasure up there?" Tiana asked, pointing toward the top of the hill.

"It will be," Gayloris said.

The answer was a bit odd, but Tiana knew that the Wisemother didn't always give a direct reply.

They walked along a series of hidden paths. At noon, they entered a small clearing. They stopped for a meal, though Tiana would have willingly given up food to get to the treasure sooner.

"You will see the treasure three times," Gayloris said after they had eaten. "The first is just ahead." She walked across the clearing to a wall of stone covered with vines. She reached into the vines and did something with her hands. The leaves moved aside.

Tiana gasped. The wall beneath the vines, for as high as she could see, was a solid piece of yellow metal. It was almost too bright to look at. She squinted, seeing herself and the Wisemother reflected in the shiny surface. "It's so . . ."

"Say nothing yet," Gayloris warned. "this is the time to see and think. The metal is called *gold*." She reached in again and the leaves covered the gold. "This way."

Tiana followed her through another section of forest. The wall of gold was incredible. This was surely the greatest treasure anyone could dream of. She wondered why she had seen no gold in the village. If the people had so much wealth, why was it hidden?

Lost in thought, she was startled to hear Gayloris speak again. "We are here," the Wisemother said, pointing to a rock cliff. She reached between two boulders. With barely a sound, the cliff walls swung open. If the gold had taken her breath away, surely this sight nearly stole her heart. Towering above her, stretching out of sight, was a shiny crystal with a billion glittering surfaces. "What . . . ?" she asked.

"It's a diamond," Gayloris replied with a gentle smile. "Our most skilled craftsmen have been cutting and polishing it for many years. The work gives them great pleasure. Hush, just look."

Tiana looked. All the colors of the rainbow flashed inside the diamond. It took the sunlight and turned it into magic. Each polished surface of the stone, each facet, reflected her awestruck face.

"One more time," Gayloris said, breaking Tiana from the spell. "Think of what you have seen and what it means."

"I've seen two great treasures," Tiana said.

"You've seen our greatest treasure twice."

Tiana was puzzled. Were the gold and the diamond the same thing? But she had another question. "Why do we have no gold in the village?"

"It has no use. But others want it very much. Some have fought over gold. Some have died."

"It is very beautiful," Tiana said.

"So is the sunset. So is a flower. So are we."

Tiana followed the Wisemother, wondering what else she would see. If the gold brought harm to people, how could it be a treasure? "Do people fight for diamonds also?" she asked, although she knew the answer.

Gayloris nodded, then said, "Again, I show you the greatest treasure of our people." She knelt at the edge of a small pool of water.

Tiana joined her and looked down, wondering what treasure could possibly be found within the shallow pond. "I don't see anything." There was nothing—nothing at all.

"You've seen the greatest treasure of our people three times on this, your First Passage," the Wisemother explained. "Think of what you have seen and what has been said. Look again. Think also of our people and our lives."

Tiana looked. The gold was beautiful, but it could bring sorrow. The diamond was the same. What was the greatest treasure of her people? Her village had a good life. They raised food, they sang and danced, they celebrated life and raised families. She looked again into the water. She looked at her reflection.

She turned toward Gayloris. "Me?" she asked. "I'm the greatest treasure of our people?"

Gayloris smiled but said nothing.

"Not just me, all the children," Tiana continued. "That's it, isn't it? We're the treasure. And the children to come will be our treasure." A sudden feeling of wonder and joy washed over her.

Gayloris rose from the pool. "You have taken the first step. You have made your First Passage. Come, my treasure, let us return to our people. If you wish, I will show you the diamond and gold again on the way back."

Tiana shook her head slowly. Such things did not seem important.

Toki
and
Toshio

By Virginia Kroll

It was spring. The sun was going down, setting the sky ablaze. Toki, the crested ibis, glided overhead on wide white wings. Farmers in round straw hats dotted the rice field like giant mushrooms. Toki flapped his elegant feathers and cried out for joy. He was almost at his home stream where he would nest for the season.

One of the mushroom caps below lifted its face to look at him. Toki cocked his red-tipped head toward the mushroom boy, and the boy raised his arms in greeting. Toki circled in a display of fancy flight to delight the boy.

Toki continued on his path through the orange and yellow sky away from the quiet mura, the rural village where mushroom boy lived. Trees rose up to welcome Toki. He began gliding groundward when his instincts sounded an alarm. Toki tried to fly upward again. Mightily he flapped his graceful wings, using all his strength.

He saw the men leap from the trees. These were mean-faced men with taut, tense muscles, men aiming pointed sticks at the sky.

An arrow pierced Toki's wing. "Ai-aaah!" he shrieked. Blood turned his feathers the color of his crest. Pain blinded Toki as he reeled in a dizzying spin—down, down, down.

A maple tree caught him in its leafy arms.

Toki heaved a shaky breath. He opened his eyes. He listened to the stick-aiming men until their sharp voices disappeared into the falling night and the air was filled with the music of nightbirds' notes.

Through the night, pain seared Toki's wing and hunger gnawed his stomach. By dawn he was so weak that the maple tree could no longer hold him. He slipped and spiraled to its base. When he awoke from the fall, rain was making music on

the treetops: *sprink a dinkle tink, spat a pat pat.*
It was a soothing sound.

Then Toki heard another sound, a dry-leaves-crunching-over-moist-earth sound. Toki opened his slender beak to cry out in fear, but no sound came from his throat. The sound came closer. Toki's heart thumped to the rhythm of the sound of human footsteps walking toward him, running faster now. *Crunch-squish crunch-squish crunch-squish.*

Suddenly Toki's clouded eyes were looking up at the rice-field face beneath the mushroom cap. "Oh, oh," the mushroom boy Toshio whispered. "The hunters have wounded you. I will help you, Toki."

Toki's heart heaved with life anew. He watched Toshio unshoulder the water pails he carried on a pole. He saw the mushroom boy take off his thatched grass raincoat, then felt himself bundled into it. He saw Toshio fill his pails at the stream and reshoulder them. He steadied them with one arm and gently bore Toki home, cradled in the other.

Toki cried out in relief when Toshio rubbed his wing wound with fish oil and slowly removed the arrow. He sighed as Toshio bathed his feathers until they glistened white again. Toki loved the feel of Toshio's hands, balming and bandaging his broken wing. Best of all, he gobbled the *sashimi*, tiny bits of raw seafood, that Toshio shared from his very own plate. Toki thanked Toshio with bright black eyes.

And Toki healed. One morning, Toki opened his slender beak and cried out for joy. He fluttered his elegant feathers for the first time again, spread his wide white wings, and soared skyward. Toshio waved his arms in farewell, and Toki disappeared into the camouflaging clouds.

Spring ended, and summer settled in. Toki took a mate. They raised two fledglings high in the maple where the stick-aiming men could not reach them. When the maples turned to orange and the rice fields bathed the countryside in gold, the young ones migrated with their mother. Toki stayed behind. His wing, though healed, would never again take him beyond the mountains and over the sea. Instead, he soared and glided for shorter spurts in the autumn air.

One chilly morning, Toki huddled in his maple. When he awoke, snowflakes were making pretty, silent patterns on the bare branches. It was a soothing sight.

Then Toki heard a sound, a wet-leaves-sinking-into-soaked-earth sound. The sound came closer:

slish, slosh, slish, slosh. His heart skipped with anticipation.

Toki looked down at a round, oilpaper umbrella making its way along the slippery streamside like a moving mushroom. "Ai-aaah!" Toki heard a loud shriek. The mushroom stem crumpled, and the cap tumbled off. Then there was no movement at all. Toki cocked his red-tipped head toward the broken mushroom.

Toki shook the frost from his feathers and flapped his elegant wings. He flew down from his roost to investigate. Suddenly Toki's bright black eyes were peering down into the rice field face from under the mushroom cap—Toshio's face.

Toki saw the mushroom boy's leg, bent and spattered red like the crest on his head. Toki gathered leaves with his bill and heaped them in a pile over Toshio's shaking body. Toki carried water in his beak and let it trickle over Toshio's burning, broken leg. He saw a smile hint across Toshio's face, and he fluttered his feathers anew.

Hours passed. Rumblings of hunger got Toki's attention, and he left Toshio's side to hunt for food. He went to the frost-fringed stream and cracked the ice with his long, slender bill. He ate his fill and hunted again. He returned to Toshio's side and fed the boy tiny bits of raw fish, as much

27

as he could swallow. The clouds left Toshio's eyes and they gleamed like summer stars. Toki blinked with excitement.

The sunset cast a rosy glow along the stream and tipped the treetops purple. Toki heard a sound. It was a wet-leaves-sinking-into-soaked-earth sound, the sound of human footsteps. Toki flapped his elegant wings and retreated to his roost.

Toki looked down at the line of round, oilpaper umbrellas wending their way like a parade of moving mushrooms. Toki watched with wary eyes as the mushroom men, rejoicing at finding Toshio, placed him on a long flat board and bore him gently home.

Toki took to the air in a display of fancy flight. He whirled and circled. He opened his slender beak and cried out for joy. And as Toki turned toward the purple-tipped treetops, he heard the faintest joyful echo coming from below.

GIFT OF THE CROW

A Legend of the Woodland Indians

Retold by Marie Frotton Began

It was in the time of our long-ago fathers. It was before our people lived in villages, in the days when they roamed the forest, hunting animals and birds and catching fish in the rivers. All day, every day, they worked hard to have enough food to eat. In spring, summer, and fall they trapped animals and caught fish to eat. In the warm summer months they picked berries from bushes, and in the fall they gathered nuts to eat. There was enough food during these days to fill everyone's stomach.

But in the cold winter, when the snow lay like a blanket over the ground, there was no fruit on the trees. Hunting was difficult. Many of the large animals disappeared, and even the small animals hid in the snow. The people knew hunger. Some died from their hunger. It was a hard life.

At the end of just such a hungry time, when the snows had long ago melted and the leaves on the trees were as big as a moose's ear, a huge black crow appeared in the sky over the camp. It circled around the people and finally flew down into their midst. The crow went straight to the chief and cocked its head to one side.

The people were amazed. Never had they seen such a large crow. What was it doing in their midst? The chief bent down for a closer look and discovered a strange object in the crow's ear. Suddenly the chief straightened up and stepped back, startled to hear the bird speak.

The crow said, "I come from your Great Father, Kautantouwit, who lives faraway to the southwest. Your hunger saddens him. Because he loves you, Kautantouwit sends you these gifts from his storehouse." The bird shook its head and two strange objects fell to the ground, one from each ear.

"This one is a bean," the crow said. "Make the earth soft by digging. Then form a shallow hole and bury the bean. When it grows, you may eat its fruit. The other is maize; it is the greater gift.

"Place the maize in a deep hole and include a fish to feed it. Cover the seed carefully, making a mound with the earth. Then water it often so the young plant will grow. When it ripens, you may eat its fruit. Store it and it will keep through the long winter. When snow covers the earth and there is no berry to pick or animal to hunt, you will have the maize to eat." Then the crow warned the people, "Always remember to save some maize and some beans to use as seed for the next year's crop."

Our long-ago fathers thanked the crow and did exactly as it had commanded. There has been much maize—enough for feasting and to keep the people fed during the winter snows and even some to store underground for a year when there was little rain and maize would not grow. The people of the woodland have never forgotten the crow who brought them their first maize. Because of its service to us, we seldom kill a crow.

The Hodja's New Shoes

Retold by Alice Geer Kelsey

Old Nasreddin the Hodja was walking down the street of his village. Each step made a sharp *click-tap* on the road. This sound was noticed by three boys playing beside the road. Musa, Parviz, and Hosen looked up to see what was making the noise. They stared at what they saw.

Instead of his soft slippers worn to the shape of his feet, Nasreddin was wearing shiny leather shoes. He was lifting his feet high, partly as though the shoes were not yet comfortable and partly as though he were proud of them.

"Good old Nasreddin," Musa said. "How happy he is about his new shoes."

"Let's play a trick on him," suggested Parviz. "Let's get his shoes away from him."

"Fun," agreed Hosen. "He's always playing tricks on other people. It's his turn to have a trick played on him."

"But how can we get his shoes away from him?" Musa asked.

The boys discussed one idea after another. They were about ready to admit that the Hodja was too smart for them when Parviz happened to look up in the branches of the sycamore tree under which they were playing. It was the tallest tree in the whole village. Parviz began to hum in a happy, thinking sort of way.

"The Hodja will always take a dare," he said slowly. "If we dare him to climb this big tree, he'll try to climb it. And he could not even begin to climb the tree wearing his stiff new shoes," Parviz went on.

"We'll offer to hold his shoes for him while he climbs." Hosen had caught the idea.

"And we'll hide them while he is up in the tree," Musa finished.

The boys laughed at their plan. Usually when they tried to fool the Hodja, the trick turned on themselves instead. But this time it seemed their trick could not fail.

Click-tap, click-tap, click-tap. Nasreddin ambled jauntily down the road, his dark robes fluttering as he swung his arms in time with the sound his new shoes made on the road.

"*Selam*, Hodja," they greeted him.

"*Selam*," he replied. The Hodja stopped to speak to the boys. "What are you playing this fine morning?" he asked.

"Not playing. Talking." Parviz looked up at Nasreddin with large serious eyes. "We are talking about this giant tree."

Musa's eyes were innocent as he gazed at the Hodja. "We are wondering if there is anyone in the village clever enough to climb this tree. Nobody knows what there might be at the top."

"I wonder," Hosen mused, "if there is anyone in all of Persia smart enough to climb that tree. Probably we'll be old men before anyone will know what is at the top of it."

"A man would need the wings of a bird to get into those branches." Parviz pointed at a raven that jumped from limb to limb, cawing hoarsely.

The three boys looked solemnly up into the branches of the tree. The Hodja tilted his head back and looked up also. He stroked his beard thoughtfully. He studied the toeholds on the trunk below the first branches. He estimated the distance from branch to branch.

"I was quite a tree-climber once," the Hodja said. "And I'm not too old and stiff to try again. That tree doesn't look too hard to climb. I'm sure I could do it."

"Anyone could say that," Parviz said. "Talking is easier than doing. We cannot believe you are able to climb that tree until we see you in its branches."

The boys watched the Hodja stroke his beard as he looked up into the sycamore tree, and they grinned at each other because they knew Nasreddin's expression when he was about to accept a dare. Their faces were solemn and innocent again by the time the Hodja's gaze shifted down to them.

"I'll climb the tree," Nasreddin announced. He began to prepare for the climb. First he twisted his flowing sleeves so that they would not catch on the branches. Then he rolled up his full robes snugly about his waist. Finally, he took off his shiny new shoes and held them in his hand.

"We'll take care of your shoes for you," the boys offered in three voices that spoke as one—too quickly, too eagerly. Was there a slight twinkle behind Nasreddin's solemn expression as he looked at them?

"You are kind to help," he thanked them as he tucked his shoes into the broad belt around his waist. "But I will take my shoes with me."

"Why?" the three voices spoke as one voice again.

"The top of the sycamore tree is very far away. You said yourselves that nobody knows what is up there. Just think—I, the Hodja, am about to go exploring where no man has ever been before." Nasreddin was looking up into the treetop—not into the eyes of the boys. "There might even be a path leading to the other side. I would surely need my shoes to follow that path."

The boys saw the tip of Nasreddin's beard twitch in a laughing sort of way, and they knew that they had lost again. Then because they really loved the Hodja as a friend, they said, "We were just pretending that we did not believe you. Of course you can climb that tree. Nevermind about proving it to us."

The Hodja gazed up into the tree as though he really would like to find out where that unknown path from its top might lead. Then he untwisted his sleeves and his long robes, donned his stiff new shoes, and walked on through the village street—*click-tap, click-tap, click-tap.*

The RICE CAKES

A Korean Folktale

Retold by C. Nordhielm Wooldridge

In Korea, years ago, there lived a man named Ki Jung. He was well known throughout his village, but not because of his kindness or his intelligence. He was known because he loved to eat rice cakes.

Indeed, it was said that the only person who loved rice cakes more than Ki Jung was Ki Jung's wife, Mi Young. No one in the village could quite agree on which of the two liked rice cakes more.

One particular evening in early summer, Ki Jung could hardly wait to get home from the market where he earned his living by selling brassware. All day, he had been thinking about the rice cakes a neighbor had promised to give him and his wife for supper. *If only Mi Young weren't quite so fond of them,* he thought. But no matter. He was determined to get his fair share.

When Ki Jung reached home, he banged impatiently through the front gate, calling, "Yobo! Yobo!" for this is how Korean men address their wives.

"Yes, Yobo," answered Mi Young, for this is also how Korean wives address their husbands.

"The rice cakes—did our good neighbor bring them today as she promised?" he asked.

"Yes," she answered—a little too sweetly, he thought. "They are on the table. All five of them."

Five! Even more than he had dared to hope for! Ki Jung's stomach was fairly hollow from hunger, and the sight of the five delicious rice cakes set his mouth to watering. He sat on the cushion beside the table and started devouring the first cake. Mi Young also sat down, snatched one of the cakes, and began chewing twice as fast as her husband to make up for lost time.

Ki Jung finished his first rice cake before Mi Young and reached for a second. Because his mouth was stuffed so full that no words could come out, he motioned for her to help herself to another.

All too soon, the first four rice cakes had disappeared, and the fifth was left sitting on the table. Both Ki Jung and Mi Young looked at it long and hard.

"I've been at the marketplace all day long, working, working, working," Ki Jung declared.

Mi Young said nothing, but her eyes never left the rice cake.

"And the walk home from the market," Ki Jung continued, patting his belly. "Why, it seemed to take all my energy!"

Again, Mi Young was silent, except for her eyes.

"Ah, Yobo!" Ki Jung finally exploded. "Since you will not let me eat in peace, we will strike a bargain. The last rice cake will go to the person who can keep from talking or moving for the longest time."

"Yes, Yobo," Mi Young agreed, with a small but triumphant smile. So the two closed their mouths tightly, gazed straight ahead, and became as rigid and still as two gray stones.

Now it happened that a thief, because he could hear no sound coming from Ki Jung's house, decided no one was at home. Thinking he could make off with some easy booty, the thief crept stealthily into the room where the couple was sitting. It wasn't until he had hoisted two sleeping mats and three quilts onto his back that he noticed Ki Jung and Mi Young staring straight ahead with their eyes open, not moving a muscle.

They must have frozen in terror at the sight of me, thought the thief. *This will be even easier than I thought!* So he carried off the mats and quilts, then came back to see what else he could find.

Without speaking or moving, Ki Jung watched out of the corner of his eye while the thief made off with his rice bowls, chopsticks, and soup spoons.

And, also without speaking or moving, Mi Young watched out of the corner of her eye while the thief made off with her jewelry and all her fine dresses.

Finally, she could stand it no longer. As the thief disappeared out the door with his last load, she yelled, "Stop, thief!"

"Hah! Yobo!" crowed her husband. "You spoke first. The last rice cake belongs to me!" But as he looked around the house at the spots where all his precious possessions used to be, he found he'd suddenly lost his appetite.

Why We Have Rainbows

A Native American Legend

Retold by Leland B. Jacobs

Once there was a day that was as bright and clear as any day in late summer could possibly be. It was a day bright with sunshine and flowers—yellow, pink, red, lavender, and blue.

In the gentle breeze the flowers bowed, bobbed, and nodded. Their colors shone cheerfully. But there was a hint of sadness, too. For the flowers knew that summer would soon be gone, and winter with its frost and then snow would take summer's place.

As the flowers nodded, they whispered their sadness to the breeze. As the flowers bowed, they asked the breeze, "Why must we perish when frost comes? Why must we die when north winds and snow possess the land?" As they bobbed, they said to the wind, "All summer we have shared our colors with the earth. We have made it a beautiful place. Why must we disappear and be forgotten?"

The breeze had no answers to the flowers' questions. So it swiftly carried the message of the flowers' sadness and their questions to the Mighty Spirit, high above the tallest mountain peaks, high in the wide blue sky.

The Mighty Spirit pondered the flowers' sadness and their questions. Why should the flowers perish, their beauty gone forever? Why should there be no place for them to be seen after summer passes?

The Mighty Spirit thanked the breeze for bringing the flowers' problem and decided there must be a change. The flowers' lovely colors must be preserved. Such beauty must not be lost from view.

Just as the Mighty Spirit was sure this decision was the right one, there came a quick shower. Raindrops fell thick and fast. So quickly had the shower come, the sun had not been hidden away.

The Mighty Spirit saw the shower and sun together and proclaimed, "From now on, for all time, the place for all the flowers in their most beautiful colors shall be in the sky when rain and sun are together. Rain and sun shall nourish them and keep their colors bright."

And so it is that what the Mighty Spirit proclaimed is ours to know. That is why there are flowers in the sky. That is why there are rainbows.

KWEKU ANANSE
AND THE
WISDOM GOURD

A Legend from Ghana

Retold by Lisa Torres

"If you have a chance to get power, sell even your own mother to get it. Once you have the power, there are several ways to get your mother back."

Kweku Ananse the spider considered this proverb. He thought, *I know how I can get power. And I don't even have to sell my mother!* He decided to play a trick on Nyame, the God of All Things.

Kweku Ananse walked into the forest and found the tallest tree. Its top was so tall that it reached into the clouds. He started to climb. He climbed, and he climbed, and he climbed, and he climbed, and he climbed till he reached the *abenfie*, or palace, of Nyame.

"Agooooo!" Kweku Ananse called.

"Ameeeee!" Nyame replied.

Kweku Ananse politely removed his eight sandals and left them outside the door. Then he went into the palace.

Nyame was wearing a golden crown and a colorful silk *kente* robe. He sat on a golden stool. He wore broad-soled sandals so his feet would never touch the ground. Nyame's advisors were fanning him with palm-leaf fans and waving fly whisks to keep the mosquitoes away.

Kweku Ananse bowed. Then he said, "Nyame, you are the God of All Things. You take care of the whole world. You must get very tired of all those people who do bad and foolish things. They take up too much of your precious time! Perhaps I can be of assistance. I would be glad to take this trouble from your shoulders."

Nyame turned his head so Kweku Ananse could not see him smile. When he turned back, he said to Ananse, "It is very kind of you to make this offer. However, it is a job that requires much wisdom. Before I can give this responsibility to you, you must have all the wisdom in the world."

48

Kweku Ananse bowed again. "Very well," he replied. "I will go and collect it, and then I will come back." Ananse put on his eight sandals and slid down the tree. He went straight to his home and got an empty calabash gourd. He hung the gourd around his neck with a string. And he put every bit, every little speck, of his own wisdom into it!

Kweku Ananse peered into the gourd to see how much wisdom he had accumulated, but the calabash was dark inside. *Aha! I will use my wisdom to find out how full the gourd is,* Kweku Ananse thought. He tapped on the outside of the gourd, "ko, ko, ko."

"Ntum, ntum, ntum!" The echo was as loud and as hollow as the *ntumpani,* the talking drums.

It isn't full enough yet, Ananse thought.

"What are you doing, Papa?" Ntikumah, Ananse's small son, asked.

"I'm collecting wisdom," Ananse replied. "I'm about to go on a journey to collect all the wisdom in the world."

Ntikumah and his mother Aso said good-bye to Ananse, and he set out. His rolled-up sleeping cloth and a small pot of fried fish and pepper sauce were on his head, and his calabash gourd was about his neck. He traveled for many days.

Ananse traded his fried fish to a hungry farmer for a little wisdom. He won some wisdom from an old man by beating him in a game of *oware*. He traded his sleeping cloth to a market woman for another bit of wisdom. When the bus drivers' backs were turned, he even stole the wise sayings painted on the bus. Every time a bit of wisdom came his way, "fum!" it went into the gourd.

Finally, when Kweku Ananse tapped on the calabash gourd he did not hear a hollow echo but the flat "ta! ta!" of a full container. He had to struggle to squeeze in the last bits of wisdom. He was ready to go home.

Aso and Ntikumah were overjoyed to see Ananse. He had been gone for months and months. Aso made him palm nut soup with large succulent forest snails and *fufu* for dinner. After he finished eating, he heaved a sigh of contentment and said, "Now I must go for a walk into the forest."

"I will come with you," Ntikumah said. He had missed his father very much.

"Very well," Ananse replied.

So Ntikumah and his spider father walked deep into the forest until they came to the tallest tree.

"Wait here for me," Ananse told Ntikumah. "I have some business with Nyame." Kweku Ananse began to climb the tree. He didn't get far because the full gourd began to bump against his belly. It made it hard to climb. Ananse pushed it aside, but the string got tangled in his arms and gave him more trouble. A bit further on, the string got caught in a branch and Ananse had to stop to untangle it. Before long, Ananse was fuming.

"Papa!" Ntikumah called. "If you have all the wisdom of the world in that calabash gourd, why don't you have the sense to put it on your back while you climb? Then it won't be in your way!"

When Kweku Ananse heard that, the words stung him—pwee! He realized that at least one small bit of wisdom had escaped his quest! He was so astonished and enraged that just for a moment he let go of the tree, and he fell to earth—plop! The calabash gourd broke, and all the bits of wisdom flew out—whoosh! They scattered quickly all over the world, and each person got a little bit.

The God of All Things, Nyame, looked down from his *ahenfie* and chuckled. "Hwee, hwee, hwee! The joke is on Ananse this time," he laughed. "Now all people can help me with my job, just by using their bits of wisdom. I won't need Ananse's services after all!"

A Wise Choice

Based on an old tale
from the Pennsylvania Dutch

By Pam Sandlin

After an especially hard day's labor, an old farmer decided that all of the work and chores were too much for one person. He resolved to hire a helper. He spread the word to friends and neighbors that he would like to hire someone to help out around the place.

Days went by and no one asked about the job. Finally, he hitched up the mule and drove to town. There he put up a notice in the general store. *Surely,* he thought to himself, *some likely lad is in need of a job.*

Several days later, the farmer was working in his field when he noticed a big, strong boy trudging up the lane. He called out to the boy to go on up to the house and wait.

He finished plowing the row he was on and turned the mule back to the barn. To his surprise, he saw not one boy, but three awaiting his arrival!

This posed a real problem. He needed one helper, not three. If he could hire only one, how could he be sure to pick the best of the group?

The farmer instructed one young man to wait by the barn, another to wait by the well, and the third to wait on the porch of the house.

He went from one applicant to the next. He asked each one about his experience with plowing fields, working with animals, and taking care of other farm chores. When all three had given him their answers, he was more puzzled than ever. All of them seemed perfectly qualified to work on a farm. All of them seemed ready and eager to work hard. The farmer's head began to ache. Which one should he hire?

He thought and thought. Finally, he decided to ask each candidate one final question.

"Tell me," he asked the fellow by the well. "How long can you plow with a rock in your shoe?"

"Why, I could plow all day," boasted the boy. "A little thing like a rock would not stop me!"

The farmer rubbed his chin and pondered a moment. Then he went to the lad on the porch.

"If you got a rock in your shoe," he queried, "how long could you plow?"

"Oh, probably half a day or so," the youth replied. "I would keep going until a dinner break or until the field was done."

"I see," said the farmer.

Finally, he approached the young man by the barn. "How long can you plow with a stone in your shoe?" the farmer inquired.

"Not one minute, sir!" the boy answered at once. "When I get a stone in my shoe, I take it out immediately!"

The farmer hired that young man that very minute, sure that he had made a wise choice.

The Badger and the Eagle

Adapted from a Native American Tale

By Donna L. Clovis

When Mother Earth gives birth to spring, all life awakens. Mountains and hills turn green and flowers bloom in pink and yellow. It is the time when animals bear and nurture their young. Life is abundant.

As summertime comes forth, the young are old enough to play and explore their surroundings. It is during this time our story takes place.

A badger cub comes forth from his cozy burrow into the light of day. His brown-and-white-striped face wrinkles as he feels the warmth of the sun-light. He sniffs his way slowly through the tall grass to the lake. He jumps into the water to play.

He swims and splashes. He rolls from his back to his belly and splashes some more. As he swims on his back, he sees a shadow fall from the sky and land nearby. He dives beneath the water, then pokes his head above the surface. He squints at the shadow upon the lake's bank. The curious badger swims closer to the bank.

"I have taken three dives for a fish and cannot catch one," the shadow said. "I caught fish every time when Mother was here."

"There's plenty of fish," the badger said. "Maybe I was in your way."

"Who are you and what are you?" the shadow asked. "You certainly are not a fish. Why were you in my way?"

"I am a badger cub, born in spring. I'm sorry to be in your way and I am sorry I cannot see you very well. I am nearly blind. My eyes are better in darkness. Who are you?"

"Why, I am an eagle, one of the great bald eagles born in spring. My eyesight is keen and bright. And from the sky, I can see the beauty of the entire earth. Above the clouds, there's endless sapphire blue, and below the clouds, there is brown and green. I can sail over the landscape and ride the free warm air of the heavens. I can fly precisely and soar in circles."

"And you can't catch fish?" the badger asked.

"You were in my way!" the eagle replied.

"Maybe if you studied the land as precisely as you study the skies, you would be able to catch fish."

"It's much more fun to soar in the sky and take free rides from the winds. I do not find the land to be so beautiful."

"And you can't catch fish."

The eagle looked puzzled.

"The part of the earth called land is full of beauty. I can feel the warmth of the sun and the coolness of my burrow home. I can hear beauty in the songs of birds and the howl of the wolf. I can smell the beauty in the freshness of the soil and the sweetness of flowers. I can play and splash in the cool water of this beautiful lake."

"And scare my fish!" the eagle said sourly.

"If you find beauty in the way of the land, the land would be good to you and give you fish."

"If you stay out of the water, I could catch fish."

"Go then. I will stay on this bank and wait for your shadow to fly into the lake and catch a fish."

The eagle left and flew high into the heavens. He made a circle, then another, then three, and dove at his highest speed into the lake.

"Eagle," called the badger. "I saw your shadow fly swiftly by. Did you catch a fish?"

The eagle landed next to the badger. "No, I didn't catch the fish."

"Then you must stand upon these banks and look for the beauty of the land. Study the water. Sit and be still. Think of all the blessings from Mother Earth. Watch and be patient. Then you will be ready to hunt fish. That's what my mother has said," the badger said, walking away from the lake.

This experience taught the eagle how to perch for his fish. He learned to sit as still as a totem pole, studying the water for hours to catch his prey.

Then, with the most precise and quick movement, he caught his first fish. Then another and another. With great pride, he mastered this important lesson from Mother Earth.

And this lesson would feed his belly for a lifetime.

The Hatmakers' New Year

A Tale of Old Japan

By Mary Dana Rodriguez

Outside the ancient city of Kyoto, in Japan, lived an old man and woman who made their living by weaving hats from straw.

The old woman, sitting on a mat, sighed deeply. "If only we had some rice cakes for New Year's Day, tomorrow," she said to her husband.

"We have fine straw hats finished," the old man answered. "I will take them to the city and see if I can sell them. Then I will buy some rice cakes.

So with his hats he started for Kyoto. It was winter, and a biting wind swept down from the mountains and cold gusts pushed in from the bay. The little old man pulled his jacket closer and bent over with his burden of hats on his back.

When he reached the city, he sat down in the marketplace. There were many people there, making their way through the stalls.

"Fine straw hats for sale!" he called.

One lady stopped. "Do you have a piece of silk?" she asked. "I do not want a hat today— only red and gold silk to make a new kimono for New Year's."

The old man shook his head.

A man in a rickshaw rode up. "I am looking for a blue porcelain jar to give my wife for New Year's," he said.

"I have only hats," the old man answered.

Then a boy and girl paused in front of him. "We are shopping for a red lacquer tray for our parents on New Year's," they said.

"That is a fine sentiment," said the old man, "but all I have are hats."

The wind began to blow hard again and the old man shivered. It started snowing.

One by one the people left the marketplace and hastened to their homes, where they could light a fire in the brazier and get warm. The old man was the only one left.

"I cannot sell hats to the wind," he told himself sadly. "And now my poor wife will have no rice cakes for New Year's." So he strapped his hats to his back and started home, too.

He decided to take a shortcut that passed a row of six stone statues of Jizo, the protector of all Japanese children.

The images looked bleak and forlorn as they stood on the edge of the deserted path, their heads and shoulders covered with snow.

"What a pity," said the old man. "They are only statues, but they look so cold and forgotten. I know what to do."

Quickly he unfastened the five hats from his back and tied them one by one on the heads of the Jizo figures.

When he came to the sixth statue he said, "Oh my! I don't have enough hats!" Then he remembered his own hat. He took it off and put it on the head of the last Jizo.

When he reached home, his wife met him at the door. "Good! Good!" she said. "You have sold all the hats, even the one you were wearing."

"No," answered the old man. And he explained to her about the six Jizo statues.

"I ought to scold you," his wife said, "but it was a very kind thing you did. It is better to have a husband with a generous heart than to have all the rice cakes in the world."

After they ate their supper of fish soup it was quite late, so the old couple went to bed.

Just before dawn they were awakened by the sound of a sled being dragged up to their cottage. They heard voices singing.

A kind old man walking in the snow
Gave all his hats to the stone Jizo
So we bring him gifts
With a yo-heave-ho!

The old couple jumped up from their mats and ran to the door. When they opened it, they could scarcely believe their eyes. There at their feet, neatly spread on an ebony-and-gold tray, were six of the largest and most delicious-looking rice cakes they had ever seen.

Then the old couple saw tracks in the snow leading away from their cottage. And in the distance, pulling an empty sled behind them, were the six stone Jizos, still wearing the hats the old man had placed on them.

So, with all the wonderful rice cakes to eat and the beautiful tray to cherish, the hatmaker and his wife celebrated the best New Year's Day they had ever had.

The
Terrible
Noise

A Folktale of Ancient India

Retold by Josepha Sherman

One day a woodcutter went into the jungle to cut firewood. It was very quiet in the jungle. Not a bird sang. Not a leaf stirred.

No sooner had the woodcutter raised his ax than—Oh! What a terrible noise! It was all around him! *Gong! Gong! Gong!*

"Monsters!" cried the woodcutter. He ran all the way back to his village. "Help!" he shouted. "Monsters! Help!"

All the people came running. "What's the matter?"

"There are monsters in the jungle!" the wood-cutter said.

"Are you sure?" the barber cried, dropping his shaving brush.

"How do you know?" the baker whimpered, squeezing a big loaf of bread into two little ones.

"I heard them all around me!" the woodcutter said. "They were making so much noise they didn't know I was there. That is how I got away."

"Who will go into the jungle to see if there are really monsters?" the tailor asked.

Nobody wanted to go alone. So all the villagers went into the jungle together. The jungle was very quiet. Not a bird sang. Not a leaf stirred.

And then—Oh! What a terrible noise! *Gong! Gong! Gong!*

"Monsters!" everybody screamed. "Run!" They all ran back to the village.

"But how do you know there are monsters?" asked a little girl named Kamala. "All you heard was a noise."

"Only monsters could have made so much noise," the baker said. "Go away, little girl!"

So Kamala went into the jungle. It was very quiet. Not a bird sang. Not a leaf stirred.

And then—Oh! What a terrible noise! *Gong! Gong! Gong!*

But Kamala did not run away. She hid beneath a big bush. Even though she was afraid, she wanted to see what was making that terrible noise.

When Kamala saw, she began to laugh. "Now I know the secret of the terrible noise," she said.

Kamala walked back to the village. The villagers were standing together, arguing and shouting. Then the tailor cried, "Look! It's Kamala. But what is she carrying? And what is following her?"

Sitting on Kamala's shoulder was a monkey. More monkeys were following her. And in her arms she carried something that gleamed. "I caught the monsters," Kamala said with a laugh.

"Those aren't monsters!" the woodcutter exclaimed. "They are only monkeys. What about the terrible noise?"

"Look what I found in the jungle," said Kamala. "It must have fallen off somebody's wagon. The monkeys were playing with it—like this!" She swung the gleaming object. And—Oh! What a terrible noise! *Gong! Gong! Gong!*

The woodcutter began to laugh. Soon everyone in the village was laughing. "How silly we were!" the woodcutter said. "Those terrible monsters were nothing but monkeys, and the terrible noise was nothing but a big brass bell!"

The Geauga Legend

By Betty John

Wa'kuta chose the swiftest of the arrows he had made that March morning. He aimed it at Wis'awanik, a red squirrel, motionless against the black bark of a great maple tree.

That means he did not see or hear me, Wa'kuta thought. He felt a warm glow of pride. His father Camingo, chief of the Eries, had been teaching him how to be silent and invisible.

"To move through the forest as one with the wind," Chief Camingo had told him, "is the mark of a good hunter. I have named you Wa'kuta, The-One-That-Shoots-Arrows, because you, my youngest son, must be the provider for our tribe. Let your older brothers be the warriors. The Eries will always look to you for food. Learn to hunt well, Wa'kuta. I have said it. So must it be."

Though Wa'kuta had not quite reached twelve winters, he had spent most of his days at his father's side in the great Manikiki, the vast maple forests that rose high above the Shaguin and the Cuyahoga Rivers. These hunting lands were called Geauga and were favored by the Eries.

Now he had to hunt alone. The deerskin pouch hanging heavy from his shoulders held many rabbits but not one squirrel. Squirrels had a way of disappearing around the other side of a tree before he could take aim.

Wa'kuta let his arrow fly. It sped straight and true toward Wis'awanik. But when it struck, it went deep into the bark of the great maple. Wis'awanik was not there.

Wa'kuta shook his fist at the red squirrel scolding and mocking him from high above. "I'll get you yet," he promised. Then he tugged at his arrow. When it came free, a spurt of clear, sticky fluid trickled down the trunk from the hole his arrow had made.

The great maple tree bleeds, Wa'kuta thought. Not wishing to get his new raccoon jacket sticky, he licked the arrowhead clean. "Mmm, what a delicious sweet taste! Almost as sweet as wild bees' honey! Why has no one told me about the sweet blood of the maple tree? I must take a taste of this back to my family. But how do I gather it as it runs down the tree?"

Then he remembered the little gourd cup that hung by a thong from his belt. "There should be some way I can hang this up there. But if I put a peg in the hole to hang this on, then I will stop the flow. A hollow reed might do."

He raced down to the swamp's edge and cut a finger's length of reed. He fitted it in the hole his arrow had made, and immediately the sweet water began to drip from the end of the reed. With the point of his knife he worked a second hole in the top of his gourd cup, tied the other end of the thong through the new hole, and hung it at the end of the reed. Then he continued to hunt until the sun cast long tree shadows across the forest floor.

He found very little fluid in his gourd to take to his family—just one little drop apiece. But he was as proud of his discovery as he was of his bulging pouch that now held two squirrels along with the many rabbits.

"It is indeed the tree's lifeblood," Chief Camingo said. "But I have never tasted it before. You have discovered a new, good thing for us, Wa'kuta. After this long, hard winter our people will be pleased. You must find more of it so that everyone can have a taste."

Early next morning Wa'kuta went alone into the great Manikiki with many elm-bark buckets his family had helped him make in the light of the fire the night before. He shot his arrows into many different kinds of trees. All of them bled, but most gave a bitter-tasting water. Only the black-barked maples gave the sticky-sweet water.

Each day he set out the buckets in the morning and took them back to the village in the evening after he had spent the day hunting. In the village he poured the contents of his buckets into earthen pots for everyone to share and enjoy.

The Erie children loved Wa'kuta's maple water so much that they willingly carried his buckets for him each day. Soon the whole village helped him gather the maple's bountiful gift. Even friendly neighboring tribes joined in.

Then one day the little green leaves appeared on the maple trees, and the sweet water suddenly stopped flowing. "We will have to try again next year after the snows melt but before the leaves come," Wa'kuta said, and went back to his hunting.

But during the hot summer months something disastrous happened to the sweet water the Erie children had worked so hard to gather and to store in the earthen pots. The sweet water fermented and spoiled. Only the fluid a few families had boiled down to save space remained good. In fact, because it was so much thicker, it was much sweeter.

Ever after, the Eries boiled their maple water down into a thick and wonderful syrup and sometimes even into crystals we call sugar.

The Eries were defeated by their cousins, the Iroquois, and disappeared from the shores of Lake Erie more than 300 years ago. Before they went, however, they had given their name to the great lake. They had also given to all people the priceless secret that might have remained forever locked in the tall trunks of Geauga's Manikiki.

Snow for the Queen

The Legend of the Almond Tree

Adapted and retold by Carol M. Harris

Long ago in a place where the sea sparkled and flowers raised their colorful faces to the sun lived a Moorish king. He had conquered the fertile land called the Algarve and for a time was content to enjoy its beauty. But soon he became bored and lonely with no wife to share its treasures. From scullery to stable, from villages to countryside, the people dreaded his increasing bouts of bad temper.

They feared for their peaceful existence each time he traveled with his soldiers.

One day he returned from a journey to northern lands and with him he brought a bride. Everyone buzzed with wonder at the change marriage made in the king.

"'Tis said his expression is tender now," women said as they spun yarn.

Fishermen gossiped as they hauled in nets filled with tuna and sardines. "She has skin white as a camellia and hair as black as earth," soldiers and servants said with a smile. "The king is happy at last!"

No longer did the young man ride through the countryside in search of excitement. Instead he strolled daily in the garden with his bride.

"How can every day be so perfect?" The queen gazed about her. "How can the sun always shine so warmly and the flowers always bloom?"

The King threw back his head and laughed. "I have ordered it so," he teased. "Three hundred and sixty-five days of sunshine with rain only to fall in the dark of night. I have ordered it especially for you."

The queen's cheeks flushed like the blooms on the rosebushes.

She often rode out of the castle grounds in a gilt coach drawn by four black horses. Women in whitewashed cottages looked forward to her visits as they baked bread. Children eagerly awaited her gifts of figs and dates. But most of all, they loved to hear her sing ballads of the North, where the winds blew clear and cold and the mountains were capped with snow.

But as each perfect day followed the next, the queen grew pensive.

"Does it never snow in the Algarve?" the queen asked as she and the king strolled in the garden.

"Snow?" The king shivered. "I would hope not! Snow is cold and kills the flowers. Here, every day is warm and sunny."

"Ah, but snow is clean and pure," the queen whispered with a faraway look. "It falls gently and settles like a blanket on the earth. It keeps the plants in the ground warm and safe until spring."

The king tilted her face to the sun. "Feel the warmth," he said. "That is better than snow."

"But have you ever felt the tingle of snow on your cheek?" she persisted. "Have you ever stretched your hand to grasp a twirling snowflake?" The king saw sadness in her dark eyes.

As the days passed, the queen stopped singing when she visited the fishermen's cottages. She ceased telling stories of her homeland. Soon she no longer rode out in the countryside at all. Her cheeks turned pale. One day she failed to appear in the garden for her walk. She grew sadder and paler and drifted into a melancholy sleep from which she could not be roused.

People of the Algarve grieved with the king. The women whispered as they worked. "He has ordered shimmering jewels to be brought to her bedside. He has ordered platters of melons and grapes put before her. But still she sleeps. 'Tis said she murmurs one word over and over: *snow*."

The fishermen shook their heads as they toiled. "He has commanded his physicians to use their skill to cure her. Still she sleeps."

Day after day the king paced on the balcony of the castle. Sometimes he stopped and stared at the craggy cliffs overlooking the sea.

"The king's sighs are so mournful the birds have stopped singing," the children said in hushed tones.

Still the queen slept.

By night the king roamed the halls of the castle. Mornings he wandered alone in the garden. He cursed the everlasting sun that made the flowers bloom and the days warm.

"Never will she awaken," he muttered. "Never will she lose her longing for her home. And never will it snow in this place of endless perfection!" He flung out his arms in anger at the loss of the happiness the queen had given him for such a short time. Showers of petals from a heavily laden hibiscus plant fluttered to the ground. "If only this were snow!" He shook the bushy shrub. Another shower drifted to the ground.

As he stared at the chalky petals, a smile transformed the king's sad face. The scattering petals brought a memory of trees that grew in his boyhood home. Trees covered with white blossoms.

His entire court thought their ruler had gone mad with grief when he ordered his sea captains to sail to Africa. "Bring me thousands of young almond trees," he commanded. He issued an edict that each of his subjects must plant one sapling. He directed the planting of rows and rows of the trees in every field and valley within sight of the castle.

The months went by, the trees grew tall and green, but still the queen slept. Each morning the king went to the garden to examine the budding trees. Each morning he murmured, "Not yet." But one day he looked at the swelling buds, smiled and softly said, "Soon!"

Before many more days had passed, the time had come. As the warm breezes stirred the air, he lifted his arms upward and shouted triumphantly, "Now!"

Running to the bedside of his sleeping bride, the king whispered one word: *"Snow!"*

The queen's eyes opened as he carried her to the balcony. She gazed in wonder at the scene below.

"It's snowing!" Her eyes shone like sundrops on the sea.

Gentle breezes sent thousands of lacy petals swirling through the air. The entire countryside lay under a mantle of white. The almond trees had blossomed! The queen smiled, and the king's heart sang with joy.

The
Fisherman
and
His Wife

An old tale retold by Miriam Biskin

A fisherman and his wife lived in a humble cottage. He loved their home, but she hated it. She often said so.

One day the man went out fishing. Suddenly, something tugged at his line, and he pulled hard. Up came a huge salmon! To his amazement, it spoke.

"I am a king under a wicked spell. Let me go and I will reward you," the fish said.

The fisherman was a kind man. Quickly, he unhooked the fish, and it disappeared into the green foam.

He couldn't wait to tell his wife about his adventure. "How foolish," she complained. "Go back for your reward." She sobbed so loudly that he couldn't rest.

Next day, he sailed out to sea. He shouted over the waves.

"Splendid fish, splendid fish, please grant me my wish."

The fish appeared out of the green foam.

"My wife wants wealth."

"So be it."

When he returned, the woman had bags of gold. But still she grumbled. "This cottage is ugly."

Again, the fisherman sailed out to sea. He shouted over the waves.

"Splendid fish, splendid fish, please grant me my wish."

The fish appeared out of the green foam.

"My wife wants a splendid house."

"So be it."

The fisherman was amazed at their new home. A mansion! It was framed by green lawns. It was filled with fancy furniture.

But still the woman grumbled.

"A kingdom," she said. "I want a kingdom."

"Wife, I don't want to be king."

"Well, I want to be queen," she insisted.

Once again he sailed out to sea and shouted over the waves.

"Splendid fish, splendid fish, please grant me my wish."

The fish rose out of the green foam.

"She wants a kingdom."

"So be it."

Slowly, the fisherman returned home. Slowly, he opened the great door. His wife sat on a throne. She wore a fancy gown. On her head, a diamond crown glittered.

But still she grumbled. "Husband, I want the sun and the moon and the stars."

"It's a mistake," he said.

"Go or I will have you beheaded."

He sailed off into the darkness and called into the wind.

"Splendid fish, splendid fish, please grant me my wish."

The fish rose out of the foam.

"My wife desires the sun and the moon and the stars."

"Enough!" boomed the fish. Lightning flashed and thunder roared. The fisherman trembled.

When he arrived home, all the riches had disappeared. His wife sat by the fire in the old cottage. She wept and he wept. But there they lived forever after.

The Lazy Nephew

A Native American Folktale from the Pacific Northwest Region

By Carolyn Short

Many years ago a young man lived in a village by the sea with his aunts and uncles and cousins. Every summer his people moved from their village by the sea to their fishing camp on the stream. Every summer thousands of salmon swam up the stream to spawn. The men caught the salmon, and the women cut them into strips and hung them on racks to dry. Everyone worked hard. Everyone, that is, except the young man.

And what did the young man do? Every morning he accompanied the other men to the stream, but after catching his first salmon, he'd slip away to the beach. There, he'd lay the salmon on the rocky shore and wait for the eagles to come.

Even after the eagles had finished eating, the young man would sit on the beach and watch as they soared overhead. His spirit soared with them. He forgot about time. Many hours later he'd return to camp.

The young man's aunts and uncles and cousins grumbled about his behavior. Why should he sit all day while they worked? Why didn't his uncle, the Chief, do something about his lazy nephew?

The Chief may have been the wealthiest and most influential man in the village, but even he could not keep his nephew away from the eagles. He knew that someday his nephew should become the next chief, but who would want his lazy nephew as their chief?

When the salmon stopped running, the people returned to their village by the sea. They carved and wove. They feasted and danced.

The winter stretched on. Storms rolled in from the sea, one on top of another. It was too stormy to fish, too stormy to hunt. Their supply of food ran low. The hungry villagers eyed the chief's nephew with contempt. Why should he eat? He hadn't worked.

At last the Chief could stand it no longer. His nephew must be taught a lesson. The Chief secretly passed the word that everyone except his nephew would be moving to their fishing camp that night. They should pack all their food and extinguish their fires. Nothing was to be left for his lazy nephew.

Late that night the people slipped away in their canoes. Only the nephew's grandmother felt sorry for him. She hid a live coal in a clam shell and some dried salmon in a box.

The next morning, the young man awoke, shivering. The fire had died. He sat up, rubbed his eyes, and looked around. No one was there. He ran from house to house, looking for someone, anyone. Everyone was gone. After much searching, he found the live coal and the dried salmon. He started a fire, ate the salmon, and then curled up and fell asleep.

An eagle's cry woke him. He ran to the beach, looking for the eagle that had called, but he saw no eagles. Then, the young man noticed something on the beach—a salmon! Beside it lay an eagle's feather. They had not forgotten his friendship. He carried their gift home. He dried some of the salmon over the fire. The rest he cooked and ate.

The next morning, a large halibut lay in the exact same spot as the salmon had been the day before. Every day the young man found something. Sometimes it was a salmon or a halibut, sometimes seal or whale. He always ate a little meat and stored the rest. Soon he had filled all the boxes in his house with meat. Before long, meat filled all the boxes in all the houses in the village.

Meanwhile, at the fishing camp, the villagers were starving. Their stomachs growled; their children cried. The Chief wondered how his nephew had fared, so he sent two people to check on him.

The Chief's nephew welcomed the people. He showed them all the boxes of dried meat and gave them salmon to eat. One of the people hid a chunk of salmon under her blanket to bring back to her starving child. When the young man sent them back to the fishing camp, he instructed them to tell no one about seeing the food, or him.

They did as they had been told. But, late that night, when the woman fed the stolen piece of salmon to her child, he choked. Her cries for help woke the Chief's wife who stuck her finger down the child's throat and pulled out the chunk of salmon. "Where did you get this?" she demanded.

"From your nephew," she replied. "Every box in the village is filled with meat."

The Chief's wife ran to tell her husband the news. The Chief told his people to pack their belongings and prepare to return to their village.

While walking by the sea the next day, the young man noticed the canoes of his people in the distance. As they neared the shore, he shouted, "Why have you come?"

"We are hungry," replied the Chief, "and you have food."

"What will you trade for my food?" demanded his nephew.

"All my wealth," answered the Chief.

The young man looked into the starving faces of his people. "I'll trade," he said.

For days, the people feasted and danced, sang and told stories. And to this day, their descendants tell the story of the lazy nephew, the one who loved eagles, the one who saved his people from starvation and became their chief.

The Ogre
and the
Monkey King

A Tale of Ancient India

By Josepha Sherman

Once, long, long ago, a troop of monkeys went traveling through the jungle. There were big monkeys and little monkeys, old monkeys and tiny baby monkeys. Sometimes they ran on the ground, and sometimes they swung by their arms and tails through the trees. All of them followed their wise old monkey king.

But why were they traveling? Was it for fun?

Oh no.

No rain had fallen in the jungle, no rain at all for a long, long time. The little pools and streams near the monkeys' home had all dried up. And the monkeys were looking for a place where there was water for all of them. They were looking for a place where they could stay until the rains came again.

But they couldn't find water. They were tired, and all of them were very thirsty.

"Oh, wait!" cried one young monkey. "I think I smell water! Yes, I do!"

"So do I!" cried another monkey. "And look! I see a lake!"

It was a big lake. It was a beautiful lake, very blue and very clear.

"We have water!" cried the monkeys. "We can stay here!"

And they all started to run out of the jungle toward the lake. Suddenly the wise old monkey king shouted: "Stop! You must not go near the lake! You must not drink!"

"Why not?" asked an angry monkey.

"We're thirsty!" said another. "All of us are thirsty. We want to drink!"

"Why should we stop?" cried all the monkeys.

"Look," said their king. "Look at the edge of the lake. What do you see?"

"Tracks," they said. "We see animal tracks. Other animals drink at the lake. Why can't we drink, too?"

"Don't you see? Look again! All the tracks lead to the lake, but none of the tracks lead away from the lake."

"Yes!" cried the monkeys. "We see. But what can it mean?"

"Something lives in that lake—something that eats animals! Let us wait," said the king. "Let us wait away from the lake and watch to see what will happen."

They waited, and suddenly the lake waters thrashed and splashed! The monkeys were afraid. What lived in that lake?

It was an ogre. It was an ugly, ugly monster. It had light blue skin and dark red eyes and sharp, sharp teeth. And it was very hungry! It wanted to eat the monkeys. But it couldn't reach them because it couldn't get out of the lake. So it pretended to smile at them.

"Why are you sitting out there?" the ogre asked, trying to make its rough voice sound soft and pretty. "This water is pure! This water is sweet! Aren't you thirsty? You must be thirsty. Come and drink. I will not hurt you!"

"Oh no," said the monkey king. "You don't fool us. You want us to come to you because you can't get out of the lake. You want us to come because you want to eat us! But we won't let you."

"But what can we do?" a little monkey asked. "I am so very thirsty! I don't think I can walk anymore."

"We are all very thirsty!" agreed a mother monkey. "And my baby is too tiny to travel anymore. We must have water. We must have this water!"

"Yes," the monkey king said sadly. "I know. We will have this water, but I will not let the ogre eat any of us! Let me think."

He looked at the lake. He looked at the ogre. He looked at the long reeds growing all around the lake.

And at last the monkey king began to smile.

"Why are you smiling?" asked the puzzled ogre. "You are tired. You are thirsty. Why are you smiling?"

"I am smiling because we are going to drink from your lake. We are going to drink from your lake—but you will not be able to eat any of us!"

"How can that be?" the monkeys asked. "We can drink only if we go right up to the edge of the lake. And if we go right up to the edge of the lake, the ogre will be able to catch us!"

"Wait," their king said. "You will see. Come, my swiftest young monkeys! Gather reeds! Gather enough reeds so that each of us can have one!"

The young monkeys obeyed. They ran. They gathered reeds. Soon they brought back enough for all the monkeys.

Then all the monkeys saw how they would drink. They knew how wise their king had been.

Those long reeds were hollow. They were hollow as straws!

So each monkey dipped a hollow reed into the lake and drank the cool water while the ogre shouted and shouted. The reeds were too long! He couldn't catch a single monkey! They were safe.

And the wise old monkey king smiled happily.